A First Book of
MYTHS

Myths and legends for the very young
from around the world

Stories retold by
Mary Hoffman

Illustrated by
Roger Langton,
Kevin Kimber, and
Nadine Wickenden

DK

For Sophie Biancardi

THIS EDITION
Editors Prerna Grewal, Kathleen Teece
Designers Rashika Kachroo, Lucy Sims
Managing Editors Laura Gilbert, Monica Saigal
Managing Art Editor Diane Peyton Jones
Deputy Managing Art Editor Ivy Sengupta
Jacket Co-ordinator Francesca Young
Jacket Designer Helen Senior
DTP Designer Dheeraj Singh
Senior Pre-producer Nikoleta Parasaki
Producer Isabell Schart
Art Director Martin Wilson
Publisher Sarah Larter
Publishing Director Sophie Mitchell

FIRST EDITION
Produced by 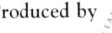 Leapfrog Press Ltd

Project Editor Naia Bray-Moffatt
Art Editor Catherine Goldsmith

For Dorling Kindersley

Managing Editor Dawn Sirett
Managing Art Editor Sarah Wright-Smith
Jacket Design Claire Penny
Production Josie Alabaster

This edition published in 2018
First published in Great Britain in 1999 by
Dorling Kindersley Limited,
80 Strand, London, WC2R 0RL

Copyright © 1999, 2018 Dorling Kindersley Limited
A Penguin Random House Company
10 9 8 7 6 5 4 3 2 1
001–307217–Mar/18

Text Copyright © 1999 Mary Hoffman

All rights reserved.
No part of this publication may be reproduced, stored in or introduced into a retrieval system,
or transmitted, in any form, or by any means (electronic, mechanical, photocopying, recording
or otherwise), without the prior written permission of the copyright owner.

A CIP catalogue record for this book
is available from the British Library.
ISBN: 978-0-2413-4173-5

The publishers would like to thank A.P. Watt Ltd
on behalf of The Trustees of the Robert Graves
Copyright Trust for permission to credit
The Greek Myths by Robert Graves as a source of reference.

Printed and bound in China

All images © Dorling Kindersley
For further information see: www.dkimages.com

**A WORLD OF IDEAS:
SEE ALL THERE IS TO KNOW**

www.dk.com

Contents

Introduction 4

The Fall of Icarus 6

The Golden Touch 10

Andromeda 14

Wolf Babies 20

Coyote Dances with a Star 24

The First Corn 26

A Newborn Warrior 30

How the Animals Got Their Shapes 34

How Butterflies Began 36

Balder the Beautiful 38

Rama and Sita 42

The Enchanted Island 48

The Kingdom Under the Sea 52

The Crocodile and the Baby 56

Ten Suns in the Sky 58

Why Dogs Hate Cats 64

The Dragon of Krakow 70

Who's Who in First Myths 76

About the Stories 80

Introduction

What's the difference between a myth and a legend? Myths are stories invented by people thousands of years ago to explain what they could see around them. In myths, gods and goddesses create the earth, sky, and oceans. They put the Sun, Moon, and stars in the sky and people and animals on Earth. But they act like ordinary people too, having quarrels and feeling sad and throwing tantrums, which explains events like the changing seasons, storms and earthquakes, floods, and volcanoes.

Then there are legends: stories about heroes and monsters, journeys to enchanted worlds, and the foundation of great cities.

Introduction

Legends are almost as fantastic as myths, but may have grown from something that really happened, which changed and became more elaborate as more and more people told the story.

Just because the stories are mostly made up, it doesn't mean that myths and legends can't tell us truths. In this book there are some that show us bad things about being human, like envy, greed, and vanity. But other tales tell us about the good side – love, bravery, and friendship. And these qualities are still as much a part of our daily lives as they were thousands of years ago.

A First Book of Myths

The Fall of Icarus

Daedalus the inventor was a prisoner on the island of Crete, with his son Icarus. King Minos was guarding all the harbours so that they couldn't escape by sea.

"Very well then," said Daedalus. "We'll try the sky."

He meant they would fly away from the island like birds. Daedalus gathered up all the feathers he could.

6

The Fall of Icarus

Then he tied them together and stuck them in place with wax to make two pairs of wings.

"Now you can fly," said Daedalus, strapping the wings to Icarus's arms, "but there are some important rules. Stay close behind me and we will get home safely. Don't fly too high or the sun will melt the wax. And don't fly too low or the sea will make your feathers soggy."

A First Book of Myths

They climbed to the top of a cliff and leapt off, soaring like eagles.

At first Icarus stayed close to his father, but soon he was having too much fun to remember the rules.

He rose higher and higher in the sky …

The Fall of Icarus

... closer and closer to the hot sun.

When Daedalus looked back he couldn't see Icarus. He called out his name but there was no reply.

Daedalus spotted a few feathers floating on the waves below. Then he realized the wings had failed and Icarus had fallen into the sea.

A First Book of Myths

The Golden Touch

Silenus the satyr, half-man, half-goat, was lost. To tell the truth, he had drunk too much and fallen asleep in a garden, so his companions couldn't find him. They went home without him.

King Midas found the satyr sleeping in the palace rose garden. "You can stay here with me if you like," he said.

Silenus was a great storyteller and kept Midas and his court amused with his tales for five days.

Then he said, "I must go back to my master. Dionysus will be wondering where I am."

So Midas took Silenus back to the god Dionysus, who was very pleased to see him.

10

The Golden Touch

"You have looked after him well, Midas," said the god. "What present can I give you to say thank you?"

"I would like everything I touch to turn to gold," said Midas. "Then in a very short time I will be rich beyond my wildest dreams."

Dionysus granted his wish. As Midas walked home, he had great fun turning flowers and stones to gold.

And everything he touched in his palace turned to gold too! "Ha ha!" laughed Midas. "Now I shall be the richest man in the world!"

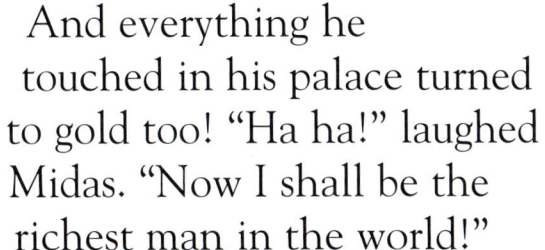

A First Book of Myths

Midas was thirsty after his journey. His wine cup turned to gold, but then, so did his wine as soon as it touched his lips. Not one drop of liquid reached his throat. It was solid gold.

And he couldn't eat his dinner because everything – bread, meat, olives, grapes – every morsel turned into gold the moment Midas picked it up.

Now, King Midas had a little daughter, his favourite person in the whole world. She came running to greet him.

"Daddy, I'm so glad you're home," she cried and before Midas could stop her she rushed into his arms. Instantly, she became a gold statue of a little girl.

The Golden Touch

Midas realized how greedy and foolish he had been. Weeping, he went back to Dionysus and begged him to take the golden touch away. The god saw that King Midas had learned his lesson.

He told the king to wash in a special river and promised that the gift would be washed away in the water.

To this day, the sands of that river have specks of gold in them.

King Midas came home to find his little girl back to normal. "I am rich indeed," said Midas as he embraced her.

A First Book of Myths

Andromeda

In Ethiopia, there was a queen called Cassiopeia. She was very beautiful and she had an equally beautiful daughter, named Andromeda.

"My darling," said the queen. "Just look at us! We are so lovely that I think we must be even prettier than the sea-nymphs."

The queen's palace was on the coast and her words soon reached the sea-nymphs. They were very indignant. "Prettier than us? What nonsense!" they cried. "This mortal must be put in her place!"

Andromeda

There were fifty sea-nymphs, the Nereids, and they all went to complain to their protector, the mighty sea-god Poseidon. He couldn't refuse fifty angry and beautiful sea-nymphs.

"The queen shall be punished," he promised.

Poseidon summoned up a terrifying sea-monster and sent it to the coast of Ethiopia.

The people of Ethiopia were terrified. They couldn't fish or go out in their trading ships because the monster sank their boats and ate the sailors. They went to King Cepheus and begged him to do something.

"My dear," said the king to the queen. "This monster is a punishment for your boasting. We must find out what the gods want us to do to put things right."

But when the king did find out, he wept bitter tears. The only way to get rid of the monster was to let it have the lovely Princess Andromeda.

Andromeda was chained to some rocks and waited for the monster to come and devour her. And it was surely going to.

But, as luck would have it, the hero Perseus was flying past the coast of Ethiopia at just that moment. He spotted the princess chained to the rocks and saw the serpent rushing towards her and swooped down to the water.

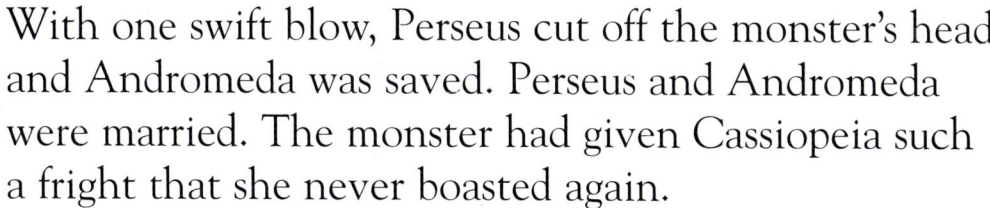

With one swift blow, Perseus cut off the monster's head and Andromeda was saved. Perseus and Andromeda were married. The monster had given Cassiopeia such a fright that she never boasted again.

And all of them – the king, the queen, Princess Andromeda, and Perseus – were placed in the heavens when they died. You can still see the stars named after them in the night sky.

Wolf Babies

In ancient Italy, there were twin little boys who had a very strange family. Their real mother was a princess called Sylvia, and their father was Mars, the great war god.

When Sylvia gave birth to the twin boys, her uncle Amulius was furious.

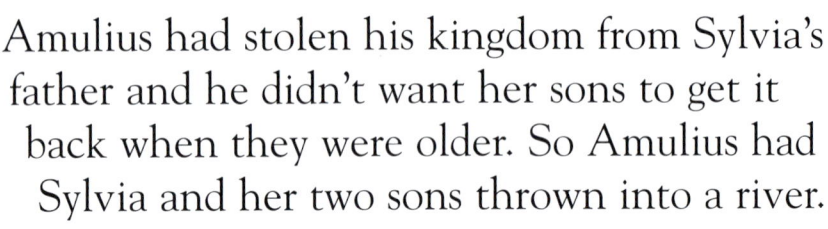

Amulius had stolen his kingdom from Sylvia's father and he didn't want her sons to get it back when they were older. So Amulius had Sylvia and her two sons thrown into a river.

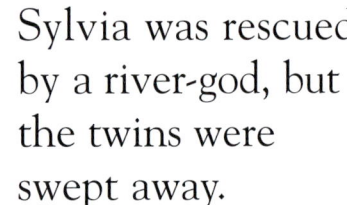

Sylvia was rescued by a river-god, but the twins were swept away.

Wolf Babies

The swift stream carried the babies' cradle far away. The waters rushed into the River Tiber, which overflowed its banks.

The little boys were washed ashore under a fig tree. They were hungry and started to cry. A she-wolf had come down to the water to drink. When she heard the babies crying, she lifted them gently out of their cradle and carried them back to her den.

There the twin boys drank their wolf-mother's milk and grew up with wolf-brothers and sisters.

When they grew up, the two boys were adopted by shepherds who called them Romulus and Remus.

The twins found out that they came from a king's family and both wanted to build a city on the banks of the River Tiber. But they couldn't agree on the right place to start building. Romulus wanted one hill and Remus preferred another.

So a competition was held to see who should build the city … and Romulus won. Remus was jealous of his brother.

He waited until Romulus had started to build the wall of his city …

… then he jumped over it.

"Hey, Romulus!" he said. "It's going to be really easy to invade your city! So much for your defences!"

Wolf Babies

Romulus was furious with Remus for making fun of him. He knocked him to the ground and the two brothers had the most tremendous fight – which Romulus won.

"My city is going to be the most beautiful the world has ever seen," he panted. "And the strongest!"

And Romulus was right. The city he built was called Rome. And you can still visit it today.

Coyote Dances with a Star

Coyote was very full of himself. He thought he could do anything he liked. One day, he took it into his head that he would like to dance with a star.

So he called to a star, "Hey, come down here. I want to dance with you!" And the star descended gracefully through the sky.

They danced and danced till Coyote's legs were tired and his arms ached from hanging onto the star.

"I want to stop now," he said. "Put me down." But he wouldn't wait till the star was close to the Earth.

He just let go and fell to the ground – splat!

Coyote Dances with a Star

Luckily for Coyote, he had more than one life. It took a while, but one day he was back to normal. And he started looking at stars again. There was one near his lodge, with a beautiful, long tail.

"Hey, come down and dance with me," said Coyote. And the star descended. Coyote grabbed hold of the tail, and the star was off again, whirling through the sky.

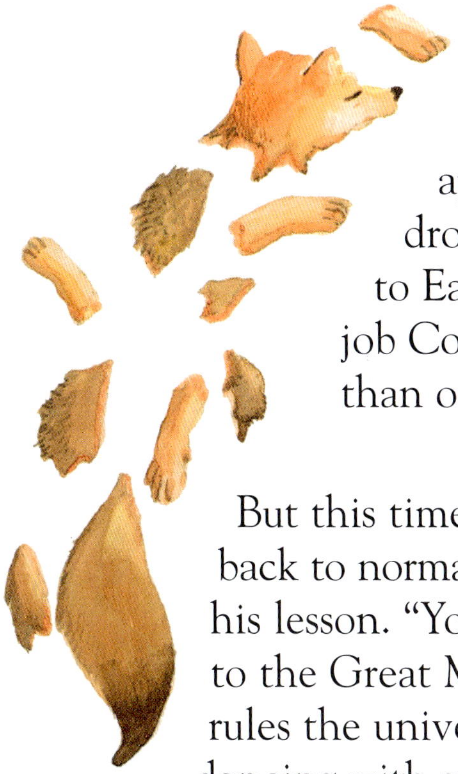

But it went so fast that Coyote started to come apart. Bits of him dropped off and fell to Earth. It was a good job Coyote had more than one life!

But this time, when he got back to normal, he had learned his lesson. "You win," he said to the Great Mystery that rules the universe. "No more dancing with stars."

The First Corn

At the beginning of time, there was a man who lived on his own. He had nothing to eat but roots and nuts and berries. And he didn't know how to make fire, so all his food was cold and raw.

The man was very sad and lonely. He curled up in the sunshine and slept the days away.

The First Corn

When he woke up, he saw a beautiful woman with long, fair hair, quite unlike his own. At first he was afraid.

But then he thought he needn't be lonely any more. He sang to the woman about how sad he was on his own. "Stay with me," he begged. "Do as I say and I shall be with you forever," the woman replied.

She led him to some dry grass and showed him how to start a fire by rubbing two sticks together.

Before long, a spark flew out and the grass caught fire.

A large patch of land was soon completely cleared.

The First Corn

"Wait till sundown," said the woman. "Then take me by the hair and drag me over the ground." The man didn't want to, but he did as she asked.

"In the spring, there will be plants wherever you dragged me," she said.

"And you will see my hair spilling out between the leaves."

A Newborn Warrior

Coatlicue was the earth goddess of old Mexico. She had four hundred sons, who were the stars in the southern sky. And she had one daughter, Coyolxauqui, the goddess of the night.

One day, when Coatlicue was sweeping the floor, she found a ball of feathers. She picked it up and tucked it tidily into the waistband of her skirt of snakes.

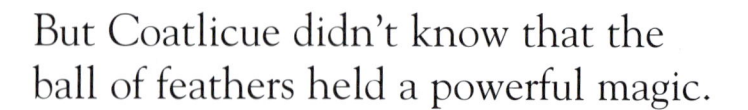

But Coatlicue didn't know that the ball of feathers held a powerful magic.

It was not long before Coatlicue realized she was expecting another baby. She had no idea that it was because of the magic ball of feathers.

A Newborn Warrior

When Coatlicue told her children what was happening to her, they became very angry.

"You are too old for this sort of thing," said Coyolxauqui. "Tell us who is the father of your child."

But Coatlicue couldn't tell her because she didn't know. All her sons were angry with her too.

In the end, Coyolxauqui was so furious with her mother that she chased her out of the house.

Coatlicue ran away from her home and through the mountain paths. But all her children were following her, shouting and waving weapons.

"What shall I do?" moaned Coatlicue. Then things got worse, because as Coatlicue reached the top of Coatepec Mountain, she felt a bad pain. "The baby is coming," she cried.

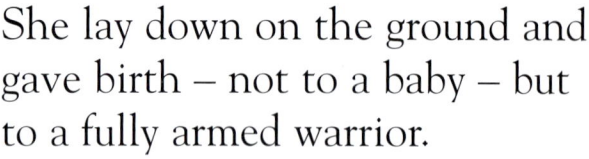

She lay down on the ground and gave birth – not to a baby – but to a fully armed warrior.

His skin was blue and gold, and he carried a flaming sword.

A Newborn Warrior

Huitzilopochtli was his name, and he was, in fact, the Sun.

He leapt to his mother's defence, because her other children were trying to kill her.

In spite of being just born, he killed his sister, the goddess of the night, and most of his star brothers.

The other brothers ran away and hid in the South.

And so it happens every morning that the Sun puts the night and stars to flight.

How the Animals Got Their Shapes

This is how animals began in Australia: first they were hidden in the frozen earth. Then the sun goddess Yhi warmed them into life. But they didn't like the kinds of lives they had been given.

The animals that lived in the water wanted to be on land. And the ones on land wanted to be in the sky.

They grew so sad that Yhi came down from the heavens to see what was the matter.

"Now everything will be all right," they said. "Yhi will give us new shapes."

"Tell me what is wrong," said Yhi.

How the Animals Got Their Shapes

All the animals spoke at once, making a terrible racket. But at last, Yhi got them to make their requests one at a time. "I would like legs," said Lizard. "I'm tired of wriggling through the water."

"And I would like wings," said Bat, "so I can fly through the air like a bird."

"Big back legs for me," said Kangaroo, "and a long tail to balance me when I leap."

"I want longer legs too," said Pelican, "so my belly doesn't get wet when I'm fishing. And a bag to keep fish in."

Yhi granted all their wishes, which is why Australian animals look the way they do today.

How Butterflies Began

Long ago in Australia, before there were any people, the animals could talk. They had never known death, but one day a young cockatoo fell out of a high tree and broke his neck.

"What's the matter with him?" asked the kookaburra. "He won't open his eyes." "Why doesn't he get up and fly away?" asked the wagtail.

No one could understand that the cockatoo was dead. Then the crow threw a stick into the river. It sank and then rose again.

"That's what has happened to the cockatoo," said the crow. "He has gone to another world and will return."

How Butterflies Began

Then all the animals volunteered to go to the other world. The opossum, wombat, and snake all hid for the winter. But when they woke up in the spring, they were just the same.

Then the insects tried it. All the caterpillars wrapped themselves up and hid in the bark of trees or under the ground.

When the next spring came, all the caterpillars had disappeared. Instead, the Australian countryside was full of butterflies – yellow, red, blue, and green.

"You've solved the mystery of death," said all the animals. "You've been to the other world and come back different and more beautiful."

Balder the Beautiful

Balder was the most beautiful of all the Norse gods. He was the son of Odin, the chief god, and his wife, Frigg.

Balder had a blind brother called Hoder.

Frigg loved them both very much. But she was scared that something bad might happen to Balder, so she decided on a plan to keep him safe forever.

Frigg thought that if she asked everything in the whole world to promise never to hurt her beautiful son, Balder would never die.

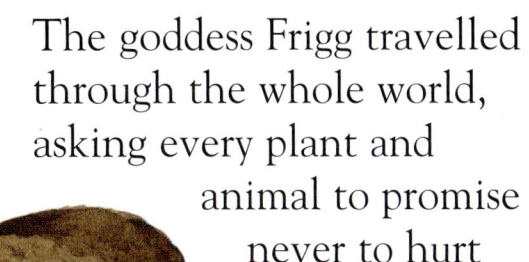

Balder the Beautiful

The goddess Frigg travelled through the whole world, asking every plant and animal to promise never to hurt Balder. And she asked every stone the same. And every metal.

She asked fire and water and the four winds to make the same promise.

Frigg thought she had asked everything in the living world and every mineral not to hurt her precious son.

But Frigg had forgotten to ask one thing. It was a plant that didn't grow in the ground, the mistletoe, which grows on oak trees. By forgetting to speak to the mistletoe, Frigg made a terrible mistake.

The gods and goddesses had great fun when Frigg told them that nothing could hurt her son Balder. They gathered in the great hall of Odin's palace, Valhalla, and made a great pile of sharp and heavy weapons.

Balder stood at one end of the hall and the gods, his family, hurled axes and swords and spears and arrows at him.

They threw furniture too and cups and bowls and burning firebrands. But everything fell harmlessly to the ground. Balder stood unhurt amid the missiles because they were all made of things that kept their promise to Frigg.

Balder the Beautiful

Loki, a cunning and mean god, knew about the mistletoe. He cut a branch of it and sharpened the stem to a point, like a spear.

"Here, Hoder," he said to Balder's blind brother. "Wouldn't you like to join in the game? I can help you throw a weapon at Balder."

Hoder was happy to have a go at the game all the other gods were enjoying so much. He let Loki put the weapon in his hand and help him throw it.

Loki's aim was perfect. The mistletoe dart pierced Balder's chest and he fell down dead. Loki was punished, but his trick taught Odin that there were some things even a god couldn't control.

Rama and Sita

When Dasharatha was king of Kosala, in India, there was a terrible, ten-headed demon ravaging the land. Ravana was his name and King Dasharatha prayed to the gods to give him sons strong enough to kill the demon.

He had four sons by three different wives, but his favourite was Rama. Rama was the eldest, and his best friend was his half-brother Lakshmana.

Rama and Sita

Rama grew up strong and handsome, and he won for himself a beautiful princess called Sita.

Rama and Sita got married, and Lakshmana married Sita's sister. They were all very happy.

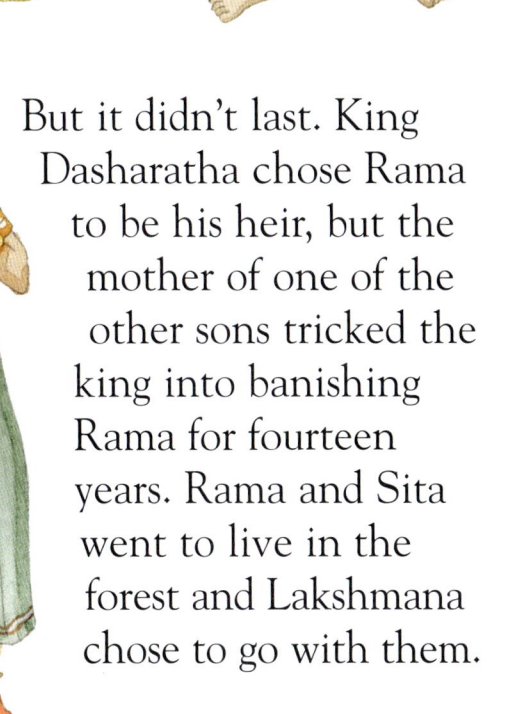

But it didn't last. King Dasharatha chose Rama to be his heir, but the mother of one of the other sons tricked the king into banishing Rama for fourteen years. Rama and Sita went to live in the forest and Lakshmana chose to go with them.

They lived for ten years by a lake and during this time, Rama killed many demons. The news reached Ravana, who decided to punish Rama by stealing his wife.

Another demon disguised himself as a golden deer and went to visit Sita. As soon as she tried to stroke him, he leapt away.

Rama was suspicious. He left Sita with Lakshmana and went in search of the deer.

Rama and Sita

Rama shot the deer with his arrows and as it died it cried out, "Help, Sita! Help, Lakshmana!" in Rama's own voice. Sita heard it and sent Lakshmana to go and see what had happened to her husband.

At that moment Ravana struck. He carried Sita off. She dropped some jewels and her golden scarf, where some very special monkeys found them.

Rama searched everywhere for Sita, until one day he came to the palace of the monkey-king. The king had a brave captain, called Hanuman, who helped Rama with his search.

Rama and Sita

Hanuman found Sita on the island of Lanka. His army of monkeys made a bridge to the island and swarmed across it.

There was a terrible battle and after a long struggle, Rama shot Ravana with his mighty bow.

Rama asked the gods to bring back to life all the monkeys who had died in the battle. And Rama and Sita were together again. Their long banishment was over, and they became king and queen of Kosala, never to be separated again.

The Enchanted Island

There was a sailor in ancient Egypt who set out on a voyage. But before he had gone very far a terrible storm blew up. The ship was wrecked and everyone on board was drowned except this one sailor.

He was flung into the sea with all the other sailors, but luckily he found a bit of wood from the broken ship.

The Enchanted Island

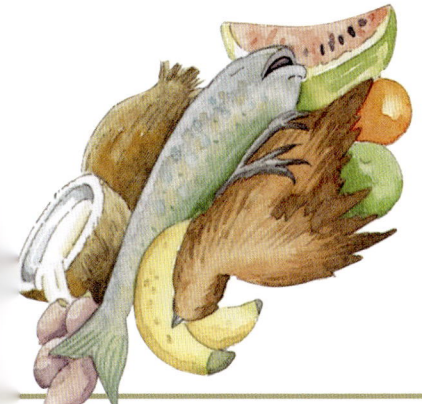

He clung on for dear life until the storm calmed down.

At last he was washed up on the shore of an island. "May the gods be praised," he gasped, then fell exhausted onto the sand. It was some days before he had enough strength to look for food.

He found that the island was full of fruit, and the sea around it teemed with fish. He sat down to his first meal for days. But before he began to eat, he offered thanks to the gods. Immediately there was a clap of thunder.

A huge serpent god towered over the sailor. "How did you get here?" asked the serpent. "Tell me the truth or you will die." The sailor told him truthfully about the shipwreck.

The Enchanted Island

The god gave him gifts of treasure and said a ship would take him back to Egypt. "But the island will never be seen again," said the serpent. And it never was.

The Kingdom Under the Sea

Hoderi was a great fisherman and Hoori, his younger brother, was a clever hunter. One day, the two brothers decided to swap weapons.

So Hoderi took Hoori's bow and arrows, and Hoori took his brother's fish hook. They agreed to meet at the end of the day and tell each other their adventures.

But it seemed as if there wouldn't be much to tell, because both brothers were unlucky.

Hoori didn't catch a single fish all day. And, what was worse, he dropped his brother's fish hook into the water. "What am I going to do?" he said. "Hoderi is going to be so angry with me."

The Kingdom Under the Sea

Hoderi came back from his day's hunting in a bad mood. "Hunting is stupid," he said. "I didn't catch anything. Give me back my hook!" He was very upset when Hoori told him the hook was lost.

Hoderi refused to have any other hook. So Hoori was lowered into the sea in a basket to search for the missing one.

He soon found himself at the bottom of the sea, in the palace of the sea-god.

Hoori asked all the fish if they had seen Hoderi's hook. At last he found one who had it in her mouth.

Of course, Hoori should have gone back then, but he met the beautiful daughter of the sea-god.

Toyotama was her name, and she was as lovely as a cherry blossom.

But both Toyotama and her father could change into water-dragons when they wanted.

Hoori and Toyotama were married and lived so happily together that Hoori forgot all about returning the fish hook. And he forgot his brother Hoderi too.

The Kingdom Under the Sea

After three years, Hoori suddenly remembered his brother and decided he would return to land and give the hook back to Hoderi.

Toyotama was sad. "I shall come and find you, Hoori," she said. "For I am going to bear your child."

Hoori kissed her goodbye and swam to the surface.

How happy Hoderi was to see his brother again! "I thought you had been drowned years ago," he said.

Princess Toyotama came to the shore and gave birth to a baby boy. Then she turned into a dragon and returned to her kingdom under the sea. Hoori's son became the father of the first emperor of Japan.

The Crocodile and the Baby

Three women were washing clothes in the river when two of them decided to play a trick on the third. They hid their babies in the rushes, then said, "We have thrown our babies into the river. Why don't you do the same?"

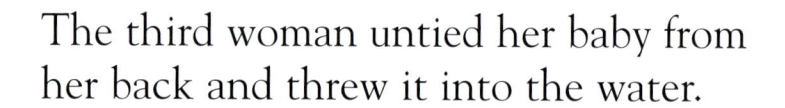

The third woman untied her baby from her back and threw it into the water.

Straight away, a huge crocodile swam along and swallowed up the baby in one gulp.

The two cruel women laughed, but the baby's mother tore her hair with grief. "I will get my baby back," she cried. She decided to climb the Paradise tree to ask the great spirit Mulungu for help.

The Crocodile and the Baby

She climbed and climbed until she was above the clouds. There she met a tribe of beautiful leopards. They let her pass because she was polite to them.

On she climbed, past birds and fish, until in the end she reached the great spirit Mulungu.

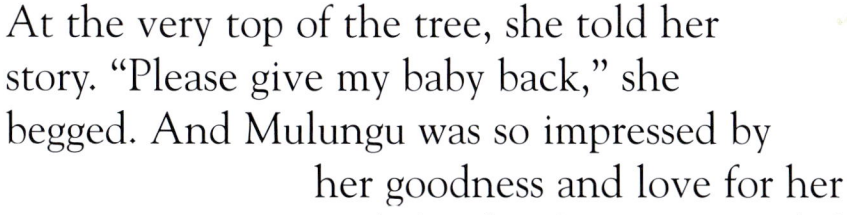

At the very top of the tree, she told her story. "Please give my baby back," she begged. And Mulungu was so impressed by her goodness and love for her baby that he summoned the crocodile and made it give the baby back.

The mother was very happy and so was her baby. The only sad one was the crocodile.

Ten Suns in the Sky

In the beginning, there were ten suns in the sky, not one. They were the children of the Supreme Ruler, the chief of the gods, and each one was a bright, shining star, like the sun we know today. They lived in the branches of a great tree that towered above the Eastern Ocean, and every day, at dawn, one of them would take a turn at lighting up the sky and warming the earth.

Ten Suns in the Sky

They did this is strict order, one sun per day, and everyone was happy.

But one day, the suns got tired of having no companions when they went about their work, and they decided they would all go out and play in the sky together.

With so much heat and light shining on the Earth, the rivers soon dried up, and the crops in the fields got scorched. So there was a danger that people would have nothing to eat or drink. Even the cows and sheep in the fields were dying of thirst. And it was much too hot for people to go out in the daytime.

Emperor Yao could do nothing except pray. And the chief god heard him. He sent the great archer Yi down to earth to help. Yi was a mighty warrior, who could split a tree from miles away with one of his arrows.

He came to the emperor, who explained the problem to him.

"Messengers are coming from all over the land," he said. "They tell me of whole forests burning with fire, of lakes boiling with steam, of monsters being released from the deeps of the sea. We can't go on like this, or all life on earth will die."

Ten Suns in the Sky

The archer Yi chose ten arrows and put them in his quiver. He went out with the emperor at dawn and as the ten suns rose in the sky, he took aim at the first one.

So sure was Yi's aim that his first arrow soared up into the sky and hit the first sun right in the middle. There was a terrible shriek, a shower of feathers, and then the body of a huge black crow fell to earth with an arrow right through it.

"That's what we always believed," whispered the crowd. "Magicians told us that a sun was just a huge golden crow. But it's black now." They allowed themselves a small cheer.

Yi was now taking arrows from his quiver and shooting suns at a terrible speed. Crow after crow fell from the sky.

Then there were two left. The emperor saw that Yi had two arrows still in his quiver, and he became afraid.

"We need one sun," he thought, and he took one of the arrows and hid it in his robe.

The archer took the ninth arrow and shot the ninth sun. He reached behind him for the tenth arrow, but it was gone.

So one sun was left in the sky, and the emperor and all his people were very happy with the result.

The remaining sun lit up the world and brought warmth back to the ground, without ever being so hot that it would scorch the earth.

I wonder if he ever misses his nine brothers as he plays alone in the sky every day, and rests in the branches of the great tree every night.

Why Dogs Hate Cats

Once upon a time, a weary traveller came to an inn and asked for a cup of wine. The innkeeper, who was a poor man, gave him almost the last of his wine supply, and the stranger paid him with a piece of amber.

"Put it in your wine jug," he said, "and see what happens." Then he went on his way.

Why Dogs Hate Cats

The innkeeper put the amber in the jug with the last drops of drink and – to his amazement – the jug immediately overflowed with good, rich wine.

From then on, the innkeeper's fortunes improved, for he never ran out of wine to sell to his customers. He lived contentedly with his dog and cat.

But one day, the amber was missing.

"Oh no," he wailed. "It must have been poured out into a cup and someone took it home."

He was so sad that the dog and cat promised to help him, and they set out to search for the magic piece of amber that had made their owner so happy.

They searched all the houses in the town, sniffing to pick up the scent of the amber. In the winter, the river froze, and they were able to walk across the ice to the houses on the other side. In the spring, they traced the smell to a box on top of a tall wardrobe, in an empty house.

They managed to knock the box down and rescue the amber. They set off for home.

But the river ice had melted and they had to cross the water.

"I can swim," said the dog.

"I can't," said the cat.

"Climb on my back and carry the amber in your mouth," said the dog.

And he got in the water
with the cat on his back.

Halfway across, the dog asked the cat
if the amber was safe. But she couldn't
answer because if she opened her
mouth to speak, she would drop
the amber.

But he asked her so many times that
in the end she said, "Of course
it's safe!"

So the amber fell
into the water!

They were on the shore by now, and started to argue and fight so badly that the cat escaped only by climbing up a tree. While she was up there, she caught the scent of amber again, and traced it to a fish that had just been caught by a fisherman.

Quickly, she caught the fish in her mouth. She ran away back to her master and gave it to him. He cut it open to cook for his supper and cried out with joy when he found the amber inside.

Why Dogs Hate Cats

So he had a good cup of wine with his supper, and he was soon able to re-open the inn and serve his customers.

He did wonder what had happened to the dog, but it never came back.

And from that day to this, cats and dogs have never got along – all because of what happened with the amber.

The Dragon of Krakow

At the bottom of a hill just outside Krakow, there lived a dragon. It spent most of its time sleeping in a cave. But at dawn it would come out, stretch its wings, and look for something to eat.

The Dragon of Krakow

The local people were afraid of the dragon and kept well away from its hill. But sometimes, their sheep or cows strayed nearby and became dragon breakfast.

So some of them went to the king.

"Please, Your Majesty," they said. "Can't you get rid of the dragon? It is taking too many of our animals."

King Krakus promised he would do something. He announced that anyone who could get rid of the dragon would be given his daughter, Wanda, in marriage, and half of his lands.

After that, many brave – or foolish – young men came to try their luck. The most fortunate ones went home with their hair and eyebrows burned off. The unluckiest ended up inside the dragon.

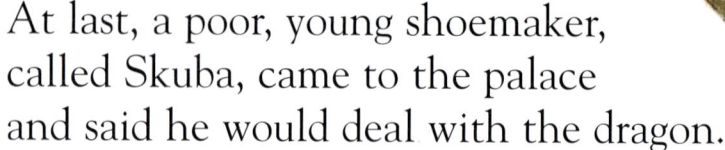

At last, a poor, young shoemaker, called Skuba, came to the palace and said he would deal with the dragon. Everyone laughed, but King Krakus was desperate. So he decided to give the boy a chance.

"What do you need?" he asked.

"A lamb's skin, some gunpowder and some mustard," said Skuba.

"What weapons do you have?" asked the king.

"Just my needle and thread," said the boy.

The Dragon of Krakow

The king gave him what he needed, and the young shoemaker sewed the gunpowder and mustard up inside the lamb's skin. He took the bundle to the dragon's hill.

Then he laid the "lamb" outside the dragon's cave and hid behind a bush.

Dawn came and the dragon emerged from the cave, stretching and yawning. He saw what he thought was a dead lamb.

"Hmm," he thought. "A nice easy breakfast today."

He gulped it down in one bite.

And then … the dragon's throat started to burn and his tummy felt on fire. He ran towards the River Vistula to cool down.

He drank and drank the river water to soothe his raging thirst, until there was nothing left of the river to drink!

But it was too late – the mixture inside the dragon had mixed with his own fiery breath, and he exploded with a big BANG!

And there were bits of dragon all over Krakow.

The Dragon of Krakow

The clever shoemaker was happily married to Princess Wanda. And the people of Krakow were happy, because they no longer had to worry about being eaten by a dragon.

The royal couple held a big picnic on the riverbank, and any child who found a dragon's scale and brought it to them got a golden ducat in return.

Prince Skuba saved all the shiny scales and made them into a pair of shoes for his first baby.

Who's Who in First Myths

Amulius — Page 20
King of Alba Longa, in Italy. Amulius stole the crown from his brother Numitor. He then killed Numitor's son and locked up the daughter. But Amulius was killed by his great-nephews Romulus and Remus, who gave the throne back to their grandfather.
Roman legend.

Andromeda — Page 14
Ethiopian princess. The beautiful daughter of Cassiopeia. She was saved by Perseus from being eaten by a sea-monster.
Greek legend.

Balder — Page 38
Norse god. He was the son of Odin and Frigg and was accidentally killed by his blind brother, Hoder.
Norse myth.

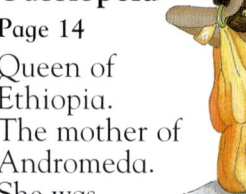

Cassiopeia — Page 14
Queen of Ethiopia. The mother of Andromeda. She was punished for being vain.
Greek legend.

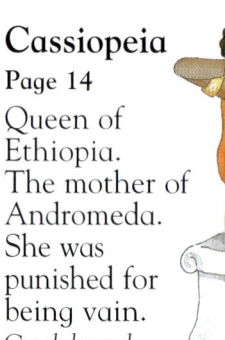

Cepheus — Page 16
The king of Ethiopia and husband of Cassiopeia. He was the father of Andromeda, and all three of them became constellations in the sky after their death.
Greek legend.

Coatlicue — Page 30
Aztec earth goddess. She was the mother of Coyolxauqui, Huitzilopochtli, and four hundred other sons.
Aztec myth.

Coyolxauqui — Page 30
Aztec goddess of the night. She was killed by her half-brother, Huitzilopochtli.
Aztec myth.

Coyote — Page 24
The trickster figure in the mythology of several Native American peoples.
Native American myth.

Who's Who in First Myths

Daedalus — Page 6
Greek inventor and architect, who built the labyrinth for King Minos in Crete. Father of Icarus.
Greek legend.

Dasharatha — Page 42
King of Kosala in India. Father of Rama, Lakshmana and their two brothers.
Hindu legend.

Dionysus — Page 10
Greek god of feasting and drinking. Patron of Silenus.
Greek myth/legend.

Frigg — Page 38
Norse goddess. Married to Odin, the chief god. Mother of Balder and Hoder.
Norse myth.

Hanuman — Page 46
Very clever and brave monkey. Captain of the monkey-king's army in the story of Rama and Sita.
Hindu legend.

Hoder — Page 38
Blind brother of Balder. Son of Frigg and Odin.
Norse myth.

Hoderi — Page 52
Great Japanese fisherman. Brother of Hoori.
Japanese legend.

Hoori — Page 52
Great Japanese hunter. Brother of Hoderi. He married the daughter of the sea-god.
Japanese legend.

Huitzilopochtli — Page 33
Aztec sun god. The son of Coatlicue.
Aztec myth.

Icarus — Page 6
Son of Daedalus. He died trying to fly with wings made by his father.
Greek legend.

Krakus — Page 71
Legendary Polish prince, the king of Krakow. In some versions of the dragon story, the shoemaker is called Krak and becomes King Krakus after killing the dragon.
Polish legend.

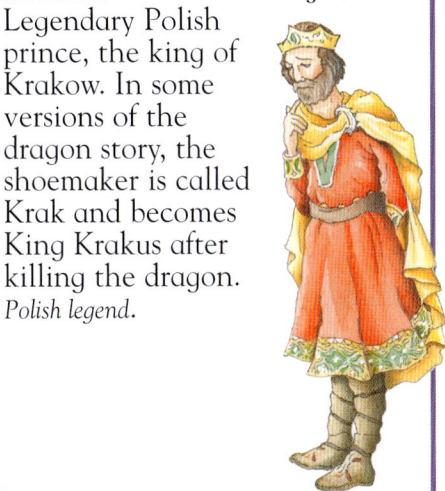

Lakshmana — Page 42
Half-brother of Rama.
Hindu legend.

77

A First Book of Myths

Loki — Page 41
An immortal not accepted by the other Norse gods. He plays tricks, including the one that kills Balder.
Norse myth.

Mars — Page 20
Roman god of war. The father of Romulus and Remus.
Roman legend.

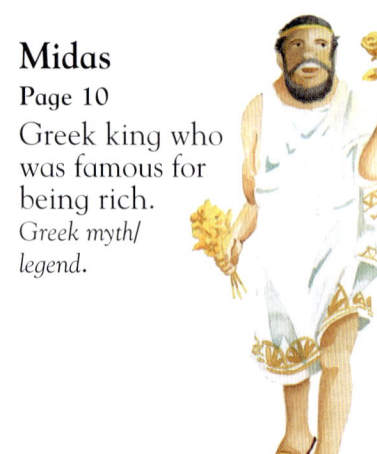

Midas — Page 10
Greek king who was famous for being rich.
Greek myth/legend.

Minos — Page 6
King of Crete. He commissioned Daedalus to build a labyrinth to hide the Minotaur, a creature that was half-man, half-bull. Then Minos would not let Daedalus leave Crete.
Greek legend.

Mulungu — Page 56
African sky spirit, who gave back a woman's baby after it had been swallowed by a crocodile.
Chaga legend.

Odin — Page 38
Chief of the Norse gods. Father of Balder and Hoder.
Norse myth.

Perseus — Page 19
Greek hero. He rescued Andromeda from the sea-monster.
Greek legend.

Poseidon — Page 15
Greek god of the sea. He sent the sea-monster to punish Cassiopeia for being vain.
Greek legend.

Rama — Page 42
Hero of the Hindu epic *The Ramayana*. He was married to Sita.
Hindu legend.

Ravana — Page 42
Ten-headed demon who stole Sita from Rama.
Hindu legend.

Remus — Page 20
Son of Mars and Sylvia. His twin brother was Romulus, who founded the city of Rome.
Roman legend.

Romulus — Page 20
Twin brother of Remus. He founded the city of Rome.
Roman legend.

Who's Who in First Myths

Silenus   Page 10
Satyr, a goat-legged creature of Greek mythology, who loved to tell stories.
Greek myth/legend.

Sita   Page 42
Indian princess. She was the wife of Rama. She was captured by Ravana the demon and rescued by Rama, Hanuman, and a troop of monkeys.
Hindu legend.

Skuba
Page 72
A poor Polish shoemaker's apprentice. He comes to Krakow with just his needles and thread, to seek his fortune.
Polish legend.

Sylvia   Page 20
(Also called Rhea Sylvia and Ilia) The mother of Romulus and Remus. She was cast into a river by her uncle and saved by a river-god.
Roman legend.

Toyotama   Page 54
Princess of the kingdom under the sea. She could turn into a dragon at will. She married Hoori, a mortal, and bore him a son.
Japanese legend.

Wanda   Page 71
A Polish princess, the daughter of King Krakus. She was famous for her great beauty.
Polish legend.

Yao   Page 64
Emperor Yao was a legendary Chinese ruler. He was known for his kindness and wisdom. He is believed to have started the first calendar that divided the year into 365 days.
Chinese myth.

Yhi   Page 34
Aborigine sun goddess. She gave Australian animals their strange shapes.
Aborigine creation myth.

Yi   Page 64
Sometimes known as Hou Yi, he was a god in Chinese mythology, who was a Divine Archer. He often came to earth to help mortals and was married to the moon-goddess.
Chinese myth.

79

About the Stories

I have lots of books of myths and legends on my shelves and am also a great user of libraries and the Internet. But some of the stories in this book I have known since I was a little girl – the death of Balder is the first story I remember being told. If you and your child want to find out more about each story, here are some other books you might try reading. – M.H.

The Fall of Icarus, The Golden Touch, and Andromeda
A good sourcebook for all Greek myths and legends is
Greek Myths by Robert Graves (Penguin complete edition, 1992)

Wolf Babies
There is no convenient source for the well-known story of Romulus and Remus, which comes from several Greek and Roman writers. I have used the scholarly work *Remus* by T.P. Wiseman (Cambridge University Press, 1995)

Coyote Dances with a Star
American Indian Myths and Legends
by Richard Erdoes and Alfonso Ortiz (Pantheon, 1990)

The First Corn
Tales of the North American Indians by Stith Thompson
(Forgotten Books, 2008)

A Newborn Warrior
Aztec and Maya Myths by Karl Taube (British Museum Press, 1993)

How the Animals Got Their Shapes
This is based on a story in *Myths and Legends of Australia* by A.W. Reed (Reed, 1965)

How Butterflies Began
Aborigine Myths and Legends by William Ramsay Smith
(Senate, 1996)

Balder the Beautiful
The main source for Norse myths and legends is *Prose Edda* by Snorri Sturlusson. A convenient modern retelling is *The Norse Myths* by Kevin Crossley-Holland (Walker Studio, 2017)

Rama and Sita
The Hindu epic The Ramayana is a long tale, filling four volumes in the original. I have relied on *Indian Tales and Legends* by J.E.B. Gray
(Oxford University Press, 1989)

The Enchanted Island
Egyptian Myth and Legend by Donald A. Mackenzie
(Ulan Press, 2012)

The Kingdom Under the Sea
Myths and Legends of Japan by F. Hadland Davis
(Dover, 2003)

The Crocodile and the Baby
This is based on a story in *African-American Alphabet* by Gerald Hausman
(St. Martin's Press Inc., 1997)

Ten Suns in the Sky
Tales from China by Cyril Birch
(Oxford University Press, 2000)

The Dragon of Krakow
The Dragon of Krakow and other Polish Stories by Richard Monte
(Frances Lincoln, 2008)

Why Dogs Hate Cats
Korean Folk Tales by James Riordan
(Oxford University Press, 1994)